For Jacqueline and Georgina,
who have waited very patiently xx — L.R.

For little monkey number two, Phoebe-Rose.
Love always, Aunty Katdog — K.H.

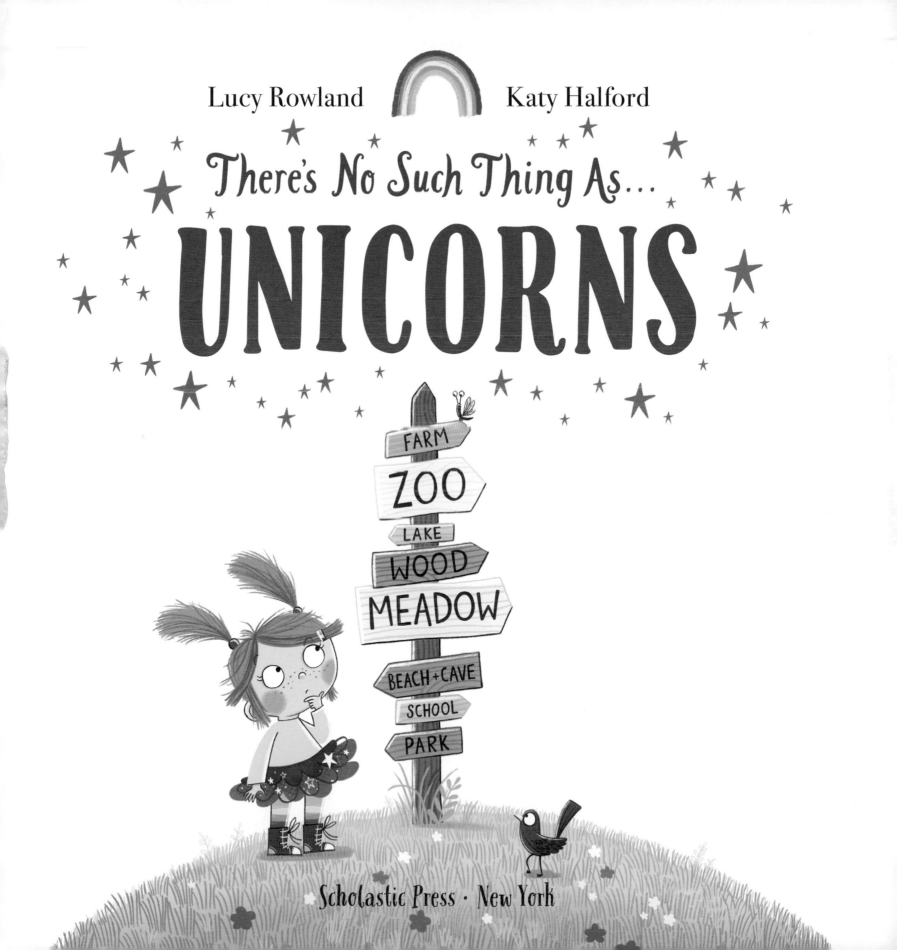

Lucy Rowland   Katy Halford

There's No Such Thing As...
UNICORNS

FARM
ZOO
LAKE
WOOD
MEADOW
BEACH + CAVE
SCHOOL
PARK

Scholastic Press · New York

"There's **no such thing** as **unicorns**,"

my brother said last night.

Today, I'll go **exploring**

just to see if he is right.

I've packed my **map, binoculars**

. . . there's **such** a lot to do!

And so much **searching** to be done so

could YOU help me, too?

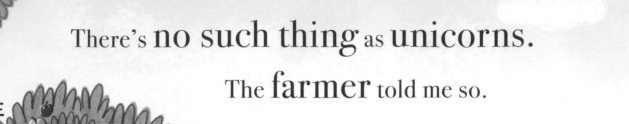

There's **no such thing** as **unicorns**.
The **farmer** told me so.

She has **a lot** of animals.

I guess that she would know.

There's **no such thing** as unicorns.

I've searched around the ZOO.

TROPICAL BIRDS

GIRAFFES
- TALLEST MAMMAL
- A NEWBORN GIRAFFE IS SIX FEET TALL
- DIET: LEAVES, TWIGS, AND BARK

They **must** be somewhere hiding

as they've disappeared from view.

There's **no such thing** as unicorns.

I hunted 'round the **lake**.

I thought I saw one in the trees?

It must be a mistake.

There's **no such thing** as unicorns.

I checked inside the **woods**.

And if they're playing hide-and-seek

they're really **very** good!

There's **no such thing** as unicorns.

The **meadow** was quite bare.

I saw some wild ponies

but **no unicorns** were there.

There's **no such thing** as unicorns.

The beach had **one fat seal,**

three **crabs,**

some **shells,**

a **starfish.**

Maybe unicorns **aren't** real.

There's **no such thing** as **unicorns**.

Next, trying to be **brave**,

I turned my light on carefully . . .

Nope!

None inside the cave!

"There's no such thing as unicorns,"
my teacher said to me.

I hunted 'round the **classroom**—

there were **none** that I could see.

There's **no such thing** as unicorns.

I even tried the **park**.

I searched around the slide and swings

until it grew quite dark.

"Oh, **there** you are!" my brother calls,

"I've looked all 'round for you!"

"There's **no such thing** as unicorns," I sob.

"It must be TRUE."

He starts to **hug** me gently and
he tells me it's all right.

We make a wish upon a star
that's shining through the night.

Then, on our way back home again . . .

a sparkle in the air . . .

a silver light begins to shine . . .

A UNICORN!

Right there!

My brother blinks. He rubs his eyes,

he thinks we've got it wrong.

BUT... there ARE such things as unicorns!

I knew it all along.

Text copyright © 2021 Lucy Rowland
Illustrations copyright © 2021 Katy Halford

First published in 2021 by Scholastic Children's Books,
a division of Scholastic Ltd.
Euston House, 24 Eversholt Street
London NW1 1DB

Library of Congress Cataloging-in-Publication Data
Names: Rowland, Lucy (Children's author), author. | Halford, Katy, illustrator.
Title: There's no such thing as . . . unicorns /
Lucy Rowland; [illustrated by] Katy Halford.
Other titles: There is no such thing as . . . unicorns
Description: First [American] edition. | New York : Scholastic Inc., 2023. |
Series: There's no such thing | Originally published: London : Scholastic
Children's Books, 2021. | Audience: Ages 4-6. | Audience: Grades K-1. |
Summary: When her brother tells her that there is no such thing as unicorns,
a little girl sets out to find out the truth and hopefully prove him wrong.
Identifiers: LCCN 2022019250 | ISBN 9781338812558 (paperback)
Subjects: CYAC: Stories in rhyme. | Unicorns—Fiction. | Brothers and
sisters—Fiction. | Humorous stories. | BISAC: JUVENILE FICTION /
Imagination & Play | JUVENILE FICTION / Humorous Stories |
LCGFT: Stories in rhyme. | Humorous fiction. | Picture books.
Classification: LCC PZ8.3.R7965 Th 2023 | DDC [E]—dc23
LC record available at https://lccn.loc.gov/2022019250

10 9 8 7 6 5 4 3 2 1   23 24 25 26 27

Printed in the U.S.A.   76
First American edition, February 2023

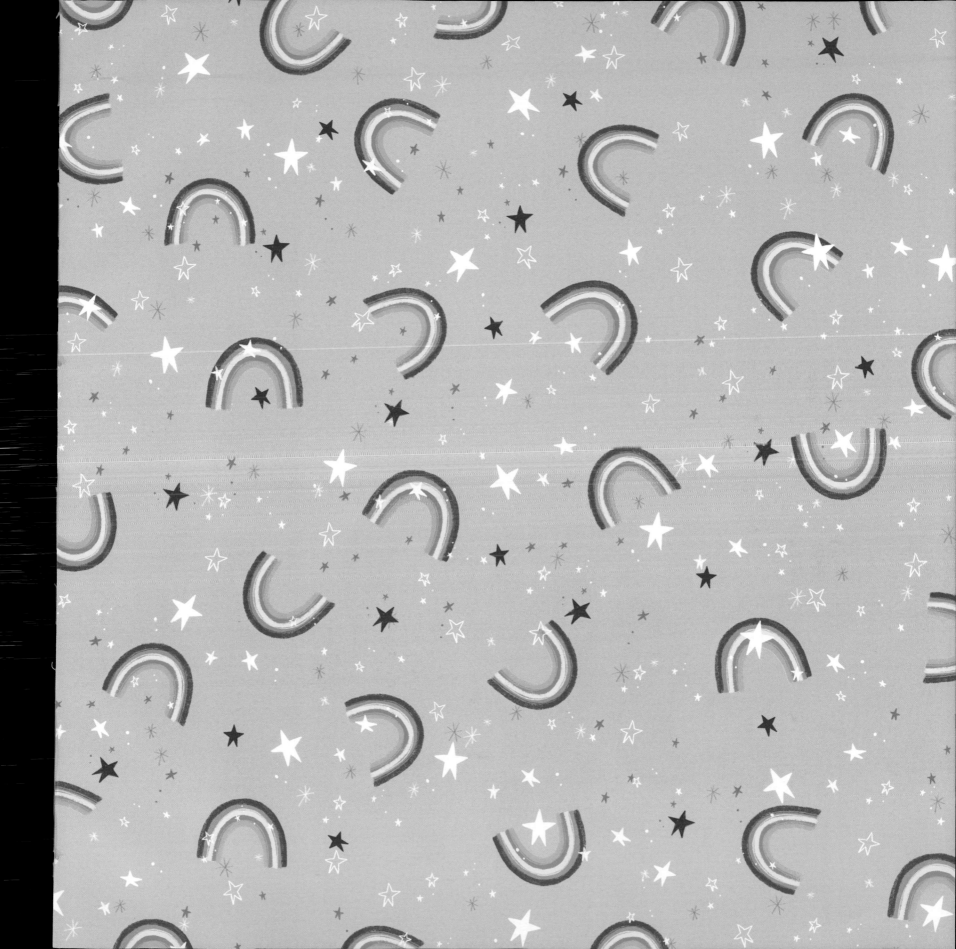